Good Help

A good name is better than precious ointment, and the day of death than the day of one's birth. —It is better to go to the house of mourning, than to go to the house of feasting: for that is the end of all men, and the living will lay it to his heart. Sorrow is better than laughter: for by the sadness of the countenance the heart is made better.

ECCLESIASTES 7:1-3

ALLAN GURGANUS

Good Help

being a chapter from
Oldest Living Conferederate Widow Tells All,
forthcoming from Alfred A. Knopf, Inc.

WITH ILLUSTRATIONS
BY THE AUTHOR

North Carolina Wesleyan College Press

Rocky Mount
1988

ISBN: 0-933598-04-1
(regular edition)
ISBN: 0-933598-05-x
(limited edition)

Good Help

For Daisy Belle Anderson Thorp
whose life is her art, and
whose masterpieces are lived days.

And who's my muse.

Inever wanted a servant to boss.

Momma grew up in a household staffed by twenty four black helpers. Most tended the yard and horses. Her enjoyment of good service got stunted early-on. The accident taught her. She passed such fear to me, her only daughter. Even at my present age, I try helping every waitress who tries serving me. "Here, honey, that looks *heavy*," I stand, sometimes jostling her tray, sometimes spilling stuff.

Momma'd just turned five when the mishap grabbed her. It proved nearbout fatal. She ever-after blamed a certain nurse, one Bible-believing older lady named Maimie L. Beech. This woman dozed off whilst minding the white baby. Accident. Child Bianca floated in a coma for three weeks. Neighbors brought casseroles enough to pave a modernday patio.

Bianca's Poppa—the 'Indigo Baron' of Falls, NC—had three smart older daughters. But he favored his unruly baby. With her now drifting beyond help and love, past the power of money, young Angus McCloud nearly lost his mind.

One poisoned baby girl, my future Momma, had been considered the local Hellion of all time. Darling, this is truly saying something in Falls NC: Brat Capitol of the Tidewater. Wealthy Summit Avenue spoiled its kids because it really could.

Soon as Bianca learned to walk, other walking and crawling children hid from her. Some parents did too. The town's firechief all but ordered the McClouds to keep li'l Bianca 'observed' after what'd happened in a flammable shed near the lumber mill. She was bad about matches. When Angus donated a fire wagon to Falls' Volunteers at a brass-band ceremony, his youngest was discouraged from attending. She was off kicking the Collier twins in all four of their shins. Hopping around, these decent spinsters asked, "Precious, why *us*?" Bianca spat back, "Go check the mirror, Bug-Faces."

Help! Maimie L. Beech got summoned, a last resort. Among certain rich folks who'd spoiled their children seemingly past help, Miss Beech was called 'the secret weapon.' Nobody knew this woman's method, nobody asked. She herself had been a orphaned slave-girl doing laundry in a Pastor Beech's home. His six rowdy children started orbiting Maimie like bees fretting one brown honey-log. She did nothing to woo or humor them. Fact is, Maimie scoffed, pinched. Kids couldn't get enough of her brimstone disposition. Maimie was the single household slave that didn't fear these devils. They sensed this and admired her for it. Kids' wildness soon tamped-down some. Preacher noticed. Word spread.

After Freedom made her a semi-free agent, young Maimie Beech found she had a skill that sure beat Ironing all-to-pieces. —Decades gone and monsters later, Maimie was much sought-after. J. V. Vining sr. had nearly got J. V. Vining jr., age 8, thrown into military school or a State reformatory or else some weighted-sack suitable for river-tossing. Maimie turned up, she stiffly tended the boy for two months, he showed first melting signs of being almost human. Now *Vining's Cotton Mill* bore a extra gilded plaque "And Son." Maimie got part-credit and a bonus big enough to help her buy the little riverside home.

Other McCloud-servants were soon jealous of a new-here woman given nothing to do but mope around the energetic youngest. Maimie was a spindly steepled lady nearing seventy. She admitted to some Tuscarora blood. You saw this in her thick straight hair, the stalky high-boned face, something in her surefooted stride. Beech's upper lip wrinkled every quarter-inch with a ruler's evenness. She wore a cross-shaped brass locket she touched right often. Her nurse's cap looked pinned to her— some unopened envelope. She was long-limbed and springy as the daily-switches she forced some brats to go cut for their own whippings. Beech jumped at loud sounds. Everywhere, everywhere, she carried her dark Bible big as a child's tombstone.

A good early question: *Where'd the money come from?*

A: *Six indigo farms, their secret-formula blue-dye, cotton sales and a small but profitable shipping-line run out of Wilmington, NC, and doing a right brisk trade 1851–88.*

First, Maimie served as Bianca's jailor. No stranger to shinnying down drainpipes, the child often slipped away. Baby Bianca collected neighbors' rotting jack o lanterns (she'd slyly waited for a nice frostbite-decay to set in). Then the scamp sneaked indoors, pulled over a chair, climbed up, mashed four spongy pumpkins apiece into metal workings of her sisters' three signed Steinway grands. The older McCloud girls cried but proved saints in not biffing little sis. Angus' eldests—in dark high-buttoned clothes—were tidy yet unbeautiful as furled umbrellas. They enjoyed just the kind of impractical tastes that female children of self-made men were then supposed to have. The day of the pumpkin mash, Baby Bianca McCloud—a pointy quail-boned crinolined little thing—took a lawnmower to the neighbor's Persian cat. She did. The cat survived but its feelings never recovered. It developed facial tics and therefore whiskeral tics too. Every few minutes, its whole fluffy head went off like a alarmclock. Something to see. Legal action was mentioned but Angus McCloud paid nextdoor—catowners fifty five dollars—held to be a fortune in them days.

Doubts were soon expressed about Maimie's secret powers. Had she met her match? Nurse kept muttering from the Bible she carried room to room the way some women honor their purses. Miss Beech stuck right in there. To Bianca, the woman quoted scripture: how if you spare the rod you just *are* going to spoil your child. Nobody knew what private punishments went on. Momma later hinted about somebody making a certain child kneel in prayer-position whilst barekneed on a purpose-fully sandy floor. The squatting Naughty was then made to pray while forced to hold a heavy flatiron level at each shoulder. Honey—what's nowadays known as Child Abuse, folks once called Just Good Maintenance.

The McClouds soon noticed their Bianca did seem tired, then worn calmer by a notch. All around the mansion and backyard, Bianca listened to Beech's tales of wicked children and harsh angels. The child's face grew sullen—a bruised, building reverence for her jittery and pilgrimish Miss Beech.

Before his favorite's accident, Mr. McCloud, Glasgow-born, figured you got pretty much what you purchased. Till then, Angus made almost a religion of Cash-value. —Hisself a foundling, he'd become a ship's cabin boy. 1839, he sailed into the port of Wilmington, NC. He liked its looks. It appeared familiar — the way unlikely-Heaven seems familiar to so many. Unnoticed on deck, a little scrappy redhead spoke under his breath, "It's on these shorres that Angus herre'll found . . . whateverr Angus here can find to found." Thirty years later, he sure had. McCloud employed over three hundred souls, he owned five freighters for transporting his cottonbales and the patented secret-formula blue dye. This local legend believed in something called The Verra Best. His brogue burred 'Verra' till it seemed to mean even more. —You did things right, because you did things once. Your every transaction and employee lasted you jolly-well forever. A King couldn't beat the quality of McCloud's major household items. What ever outranks the verra best? Made you a potentate on Earth—and certainly in Falls. Your four daughters: princesses exempt from everything but Poppa's treats. Angus' favorite hymn: *Under His Wing, Everything Prospers*. Of McCloud, locals said, "Whatever the rogue touches . . ."

Five years before Bianca's mishap, Angus came inland from coastal Indigo-growing, home to hear his oldest girls play six-hand pieces in their teacher's parlor. The elder sisters McCloud were then real young but musically already mighty good. Angus felt it. Though he lacked formal education, Angus—with his pure pitch for quality—knew this in the very gristle of his kilt-worthy calves. Family talent called for 'seed money.' The man didn't even wait on recital-applause to peter out, he bounded right toward the telegraph office. Angus, man of action—distant

acquaintance of his idol, Mr. Carnegie—wired direct to Steinway & Sons in New York City, NY. By next train—causing
great interest at Falls' little station—here came three matching
ebony/ivory concert-grands in crates of boatsized and sea-
worthy-looking blond wood. A minor Steinway cousin actually
rode along to 'install' the things. Such are the benefits, child,
of buying only the you-know-what. A party at the house was
wrote up in *The Falls Herald Traveler*, photos inclusive. I've seen
these yellowed newsprint pictures of my squaredjaw grandpa
and his plain musical girls. The Indigo Baron is shown being
taught scales at three different concert-grands by three thin
gifted daughters. One giggler hides her face behind a raised
hand. Another uses sheet music plainly marked *Humoresque*, that
camera-shy.

Determined to succeed here, Famous Maimie Beech soon
doled out unexpected treats for good behavior. She'd granted
just such privileges at earlier homes, even to her little white
boys. For some reason, they loved it too: Beech let them plait
her silver-black hair. In backyard sun, Nurse unpinned her
cap, set it atop her Bible. She pivoted Bianca on a high stool
opposite and child fingers were soon maundering all over a
dignified woman's knobbly head. Senior McClouds and three
older girls smirked, worried, from their house of windows. Miss
Maimie rested down there in daylight, patient, nodding forward
like some African-and-Tuscarora elder saying Yes. She spoke
lanyard-hints as cornrows sprouted off of her. Beech's hairdo—
under Bianca's loving if stubby touch—come out somewhere
betwixt Medusa and a maypole.

Nurse and girl soon set to work on one another. Seeing this
felt wonderful if creepy. Maimie would brush Bianca's mud-rich

curls around a long expert black finger. Maimie tallied curls aloud like treasure. Bianca would quote rhymes she loved to scramble, "King is in the counting house, counting out his honey. Queen is in the parlor, eating bread and mon-ey." The brat— tongue pressed between baby teeth—improved Maimie's hair into a mass of plaits each ending with its own rag bow. Miss Beech's scalp soon looked to be some dandelion seed-puff sprouting kites-tails.

You saw this talkative pair enjoying long strolls across the county—(leathery-black six foot one/ marshmallow-pale three foot two, hand-in-hand arms swinging). Maimie, nodding toward bees, mud, hogs, explained: "What'd I tell you? 'Earth is the Lord's and the fulness thereof'. It *planned*."

After hiking beside the bright river, Bianca rushed home with major news: Jesus could walk on any water He chose and whenever He liked, couldn't He, Maimie, hunh? tell them . . . they don't know *any*thing. —Maimie, pure authority, nodded. Onct. Though the McClouds had surely heard about His Knack for the Bouyant—why did it seem like Maimie'd just made it up? And if she had, who here would contradict her?

If Bianca made a clover-bracelet for Nanny, Beech wore the thing till you found its last brown twigs sprinkling the mansion's oriental rugs. Nurse and child settled in backyard clover, shoo-ing away bugs, weaving jewelry for each other. The Indigo Baron wandered out, smiled down. "Ye take bees for instance," he began. Beech, somber, nodded. Angus asked if his favorite ladies knew: bees weren't even native to North America but, like him, came over on a boat. Like him, they soon slipped free,

diversifying, which meant 'branching out.' By 1750, bees still hadn't buzzed beyond the River Susquehana. But Indians soon called them "white man's flies." Indians learnt that such bugs moved 100 miles in advance of the troublemaking Westbound settlers. Fact.

Maimie sat here, appearing knowing, nodding but amazed. She took this bug-news right downhill to friends. Bees? — they asked — brung across the water in rope hives — captive as slaves? Whites shipped-in America's every bee and black and bird too? Hogwash. Nobody believed Maimie. Which only made The Mansion McCloud mean more to her.

On Bianca's bad days, Beech handfed the girl. You'd walk in, you'd hear this seemingly joyless old woman stifle certain nasal buzzing-sounds, a spoon had just been flying around one crimped pretty mouth. Maimie hushed saying, "Miss Flower? Open Up. It's Me. Here Come You Main Admirer, Marse BumberBee . . ." Feeling your presence, child and nurse would practically leap. Bianca gulped down that spoonful so quick, she chewed hard, nervous as if caught at spy-activity or kissing.

After three smoke-free weeks, Beech invented a extra treat for polite little girls: they got to go downtown with Maimie's five best womenfriends: Saturday lotion-and-notion shopping at the Woolworth's Store, hooray! Maimie called her favorites The Sisters. They were Beech's age or younger but their shapes bosomed where hers slatted. These ladies were as hardworking and faintly medicinal as fully respectable and semi-religious as their boned-corsets. They moved in a talcumed pigeonbreasted rack, all talking at once side-by-side under similar wonderful hats. You saw their dark cluster windowshopping, led by one bossy pointy white-star of a child. Bianca, meeting whites she knew (most everybody) loved introducing all of Maimie's friends by name and very slow. Just more of her mischief.

—The girl now got to hold Beech's hand throughout dinner. Nurse supervised each spoonful, she napkined Baby's mouth clean. Even when the Governor came for Christmas, Maimie was allowed to sit right at table. Otherwise, Bianca flat shrieked.

Elder McClouds did feel twinges of jealousy, they admitted these but only in jokes. You almost missed Bianca at her most over-wound. Still, there were reassuring flareups. Especially if Cook—against strict Angus-orders—left out tempting kitchen matches. But, four months of Maimie: and Bianca started seeming like somebody nicer, if maybe somebody else, somebody *less*. Four months' Jesus tales offered like bribes of promised powers, four months' stern hypnotizing care and feeding— ("Open up, it's me"). Sure looked like Nanny'd half-tamed Summit Avenue's champion Rounder.

To his paneled upstairs-study, Angus summoned this miracle-worker. He sat toying with a inkwell made from twelve deer-hooves all on point. Behind his massive desk, in glassy golden frames—a fine collection of arrowheads—arranged on honey-colored velvet, by size like money.

"Come in," he admired Beech's strange heron-long limbs, the silver hair kept seriously knotted behind her like some hostage that—if not watched—might try some funny-business. Angus McCloud looked straight into her black Bible of a face.

He asked Beech to sit, please. She would not. She seemed to expect reprimand. Instead Angus smiled. The fellow dispensed charm like twenty-percent interest accumulated-daily. He handed Beech a blue business-envelope. "Your bonus for managing . . . her. But, tell me, Miss. —Off the record-like, how do ye *do* it?" It was his favorite question. He put it to many men and a few women. Asking this, Angus always seemed to beg for some sexual-type favor, his eyes twinkled that much, you felt his palms were sweating and God knows what else. The world was a secret formula like his personally-improved richly-rewarding powder for home-Indigo-dying. When it came to necessary celestial blue, he'd cornered the international market. — The man usually got a answer.

Maimie L. Beech met his gaze with a stare that was a dye: a stare too darkly like Angus' own to be transparent till it dried later—permanent. Looking into these jet eyes—Angus saw one word waiting in each slot: "Patent" "Pending." He nodded, touched the inkwell's doe cuticles, for luck. He felt the washing joy of it—Beech too was his, the verra best.

This woman's lot in life might prove real dicey, but—given that—she knew her value absolutely. McCloud leaned forward, reviewing the amount he'd stuffed in her envelope, enough? "*How?*", he was still waiting.

She studied her dry hands. "You maybe after Maimie's secret, sir? — Don't half-know it my own self. Maybe that the secret. Got something to do with remembering what worked last time. — Sir, could-be it just come from Maimie's having . . . you know — Talent?"

He laughed hard enough to slap his upper leg, causing the deer-hoof thingie to skitter over desktop, spilling not a drop of ink. This let Miss Beech risk one pleased snort, and gnaw slightly on her lower lip.

"We'rre going to get along just fine here. Sense of self-wrath. Nothing like it, Beech. Hold onto that, ye hear me?"

Came shouts from downstairs. Whilst Maimie let herself be buttered-up with flattery and cash, Bianca'd requested the head-gardener's six children to please strip naked. Her being the boss' kid, they did so. Bianca next locked them into a gazebo. She set it cautiously afire. Dragged up to Poppa's study, Bianca was soon being scolded by her folks, loud, "Why? Tell us *why*?"

Without knocking, Maimie rushed in. The blue envelope still plugged her uniform's breastpocket. She posed—arms outstretched—between the girl and parents. Everyone acted startled by her doing this—especially Beech herself. She answered The Indigo Baron's dangling question. "*Why?* Cause of Marse Satan. He *after* her. —Times, my baby here just feel so left out, them three sisters in a clump. Satan got *His* Eye on her—and, I tell you: she *shy.*"

Hid behind a white uniform, the child grabbed its starchy hem. Tears came to her great eyes, she tried blotting these onto Maimie's crackling whites. The cloth was too stiff for absorbing much, teardrops rolled as if down plaster. —But, listening, Baby Bianca suddenly found she *was.* That. That Maimie'd said. —Only Maimie Beech truly knew her.

One of Angus' competitors tried luring Beech away, hoping she'd come 'break' his own namesake scamp and son. He offered Maimie a goodly raise—she snitched to Angus. A lover of loyalty, McCloud gave her this exact amount right then and out-of-pocket. Bianca now semi-behaved. Maimie's love had done it. Miss "Secret Weapon" knew no name for her secret weapon. Talent? No, more Love.

Her brats shaped up because Beech got them totally used to her own terrible complete attention. When she arrived mornings, kids could spend thirty minutes telling Maimie what she'd missed since they spoke last night. She taught them to mistrust their little playmates and everybody but the Need itself. She then met the Need completely. Everything Beech knew and

guessed, she told them. Her earnestness, they felt. Kids met it
with their own. In these soft spoiling households uphill, she
offered them a single certainty, one gauging straight-edge.
Maimie then scared her brats: they might lose their Maimie's
love. How would they like *that*, hunh? Who would they have
then? —Her love was strict as the Old Testament contract. God
often told his chosen children, 'I'll call you "chosen" if you
choose Me back . . .' And if not, His brood got extensive wilder-
ness, boils, bears, bugs, the deaths of favorite children. Maimie's
love, like His, kept a flashy mirrored sweetness spelled across
its front. (This, the hiring parents saw). But, behind, you found
a hundred slapped-on crusted layers of black-lead. And yet, this
very blackness made the mirror mirror.

Maimie was a strict addiction for which there won't a known
cure. None except her kids' outgrowing it, their being packed,
weeping, off to school. Children soon found: learning to read
was not a fair exchange for having been so lovingly decoded
under Beech's complete attention all those years.

Thanks to Bianca's smoothing-off, Maimie's reputation now
lifted past nanny, more towards Governess almost.

Like many of us, this woman worked hardest to hide one
precious secret—and it was the very secret everybody knew
about her first. No fair.

Arriving at McCloud's hiring interview, Beech hand-delivered fourteen excellent references. But these were notes she
couldn't read and, see, sugar, that's the secret. One letter claimed:
"Beech is a genius with children. My little Sandra called *her*
'Mother' first and, though my blood just absolutely positively
boiled, I saw how, in most ways which mattered, Maimie L.
actually was, alas. So be it."

Maimie Beech's major vanity? pretending she 'had' reading. (Some letters she herself handed Angus lightly mentioned this.) He instructed others in the house never to tease poor Beech about it.

Like I already told you, she carried her Bible everywhere, often opening and closing it, glowering around, daring anybody's doubt. She used The Book as her moral-guide but, too, her pedigree in these fine homes.

Prior to doing-for one self-styled Baron of the storebought color Blue, Beech had served born blue-bloods. These aristocrats pinched pennies, tried saddling Beech with changing brats' diapers *and* washing them. "Plenty talented *launder*esses around here," she threatened quitting every time.

But not in Angus McCloud's openhanded home. Everything he touched . . . From Maimie's first day on the job, his 40-room house—with its stainedglass, its mantels like altars—seemed almost a weekday church, some church you'd never have to leave. "McClouds' Mansion"—it sounded worthy of the 100 Psalms that Beech had memorized. Corridor-walls were paved with thirty paintings of one castle. The place rang all day with three pianos, players good and getting better. Sky-lighted rooms sprouted potted palms even taller than Miss Maimie. Though Maimie knew that the word 'Psalms' had more sighs in it than Palms did, she'd seen such plants in Sunday School lithos. She let herself enjoy blending the Bible with this house. Before the accident, while chasing Bianca through downstairs chambers, Beech seemed to aim toward palms, smiling, eyes-shut as stray fronds whisked her face. On the huge stairwell, (a makeshift pulpit when won't nobody around) she mumbled the sweeter Psalms. She recollected her favorite book's incense, its cedar tabernacles and marble steps, its chimes, the pretty-sounds of captive-nations' native-tongues offering praise to the Lord.

When Angus came inland from Indigo growing, he entertained local mayors and some foreign guests. French was sometimes talked at dinner. Maimie listened at the cellos sawing underneath French's surface jabber. Working in five decades of rich folks' homes, Beech's manner had slowly changed. She now kept her long neck extended at a haughty angle. Her pleated face stayed wide-open with a look of full entitlement. At table, she was spared having to speak the native tongue of strange nations herself. This way, she could just enjoy the sounds — follow them from mouth to mouth. (Letters printed in Maimie's Bible — the anti-like dots and dragon-fly squiggles — looked to her lots more like choirbook Sheet Music than signs for plain dull English. To Beech's ear, French sounded much more Bibledays-Oriental.) She sat here, awestruck but contained, following its music back and forth. For Beech, French became the official Psalmish gong-and-tinkle she heard steadily belling in her head.

And Little Bianca eating right here — one hand stowed safe in Beech's — this darling babe-and-suckling spoke the holy tongue.

To folks most interested in rightful-owners' control, parenthood can be the hardest job of all.

Later, waiting to know if his high-tempered pet would live or be a vegetable or what, handsome Angus McCloud lunged around the overdecorated home. He avoided a second-floor where doctors buzzed near one baby swollen unrecognizable. Experts wore dark wasp-waisted coats. They'd buggied from far-off Richmond. Till now Angus had believed a person got what a person paid for. The oldest daughters hunted their addled

Poppa floor-to-floor. Since the accident, girls wore black full-
time. They'd sacrificed their major joy: they locked the lids of
three massive pianos. Household mirrors were covered with jet
crêpe. Angus' wife and elder girls found him crouched alone in
the attic. Poor man was slowly tapping his right temple against
one wooden upright. Strapping McCloud then galloped downstairs, he yanked velvet drapes off windows in thirty nine steep
and perfect rooms. "Light," he called loud. "It's light she'll be
needing more of." He didn't blame skinny zealous Maimie L.
Beech for his daughter's accident, though the culprits had been
black as Miss Beech. Nurse could be heard now weeping out
in the garden house, tearing strips from her white uniform ("I
won't asleep, just resting my eyes after four hours' Bible-read-
ing"). Angus' womenfolk followed him chamber to chamber as
he ripped down curtains. Daylight showed rooms full of floating
dust—gold, yes, but gnat-like—a terrible corruption working
everybody's air. "Will ye look at it all," he studied motes. "Two
dozen people cleaning a house and they canna keep out pieces
this size? —No wonder."

Loved ones allowed him this temporary madness, just the
way they'd admired his earlier gift for managing.

('*Let* him'—for some ladies, it's a whole philosophy of life.)

Angus respected America's Indians ("Ye have to hand it to
them"). Angus praised Beech in front of company and mentioned
her Tuscarora forebears: chieftans and lairds, no doubt. —How
could Maimie fall from being so wedged and high-up—already
chapter and verse—in The House of Palms? Child, I'm getting
to the accident and lapse.

Like lots of religious unschooled folks in those days—Maimie'd
memorized well over a third of the Holy Scriptures. But when

quoting from memory, she preferred to fake a somber reading of it. Didn't matter if her selection came from Genesis or Revelation—Maimie always opened The Book midway to Psalms. At impossible speed, her finger blurred over printed lines. She sometimes paused, rubbing her eyes the way she'd noticed other readers do. Maimie Beech seemed to feel that reading—with its joys and power—must be very thrilling but mighty wearing on you. Jealous McCloud servants said they'd often seen Beech check the gold cross engraved across her Bible's front. This was her guide in holding the book right-side up. If the cross' T-bar was near the top, she knew she was safe from being discovered. Then her deep voice spoke God's word with fresh, level authority.

Before the trouble, Maimie and her Bible arrived to work hours-early. Long before Bianca woke around eleven, here came the black spinster armored in the crispest of white uniforms. She fondled the brass-cross bobbing at her throat. She forever wore that perched unaddressed-envelope of a nurse's cap. While tiptoers waited for the baby-of-the-house to rise, Cook let Maimie go sit in a place of honor, on the low three-legged in the stove's corner of the kitchen. Maimie's outfit was so starched, the first time she sat each day, you heard her break like pasteboard eggcartons.

She could rest over there for the longest time, staring down into a Bible big as any cookbook. Other servants sniggered. The chief gardener sometimes asked, "What *you* studying so hard today, Miss Famous Maimie Beech?" And—convicted—furious, without even lifting her head, the woman would suddenly spout four-minutes-worth of Leviticus, citing chapter and verse, finger blurring at a angel's speed over one page of Psalms. She seemed to consider that a book was like a bucketful of water—pretty much the same contents floated on its top as on its bottom. Dip in anyplace, all water. The text she wanted would rise, up up

through pages — drawn to the bait and lure of so hard-working a fingertip. Maimie got no credit for these feats of memory. She could sure concentrate. The selfsame focus she usually pinned on some scared flattered child, Beech now pegged square upon one page. The old woman paused only to massage strained eyes. She did it with such conviction, child, you found: your own had started burning.

In accepting this job, she'd told Angus, "Can't stay here long. Maimie likes them young."

Miss M. L. Beech always gave notice the day her babies turned six. Whitefolks believed Maimie'd just specialized in toddlers. But, truth is, she couldn't bear it when the children found her out.

Till school spoiled things, Maimie might sit — with some beautiful picturebook opened in her lap, a living baby tucked snug under either arm and — free as air or water — spin out any tale she chose. It felt like swimming and walking at the self-same time — a promenade along some river's glassy lid. Her lore was partly fairy-tales like one about a poppa-king whose golden touch proved butterfingered. Her lore was partly Bible rehash, part neighborhood-gossip from Baby Africa downhill, partly whatever stepping-stone-footholds the pretty pictures gave. Her finger was careful to skim to and fro, fro and to — a dorsal fin keeping her afloat. Beech's tales oftimes starred little dervishes she'd tended at other rich white homes in Falls. Her latest charges felt right honored to join a list of local children already so famous they'd been wrote up in national books.

Years back, a child Maimie'd shepherded through six years and thousands of changed-diapers — betrayed her. This blond-ringleted boy was the first to do so: She never planned to live through that again.

He sat listening—he watched her needling clockly finger move over the dark wasp-shapes swarming in rows, shapes she'd patiently explained to him were Letters. He had only been a schoolboy for six weeks. He piped loud in front of adults, "*That's* not what this book says, Maimie. You just make it up. I think you made up every book you ever told me. Did you, Maimie, hunh?" She smiled at him, tears stood thick as lenses in her either pouchy eye. Come morning she politely resigned, moving next-door to the neighbor's brandnew baby, a baby who'd admire and forgive Maimie Beech till school unlocked the betraying mystery of a black-and-white page.

Maimie might have stayed the honored servant in one home forever. She might've lived on long after the household-children grew up and moved out. But she felt determined: learning to read by *seeming* to read. That and some restless curiosity kept her changing jobs every six years, minimum. Maimie'd considered asking one trusted employer to please help her learn her letters. Beech knew how avid, grand and Old Testament her own mind was. She surely had the deepest *will* to know. But asking meant admitting, didn't it? Doesn't it always? Bosses would find: she'd been lying all along—they'd go and tell their children (hers). False-reading was Maimie L. Beech's only lie. As a serious Christian woman—she suffered for it daily.

A gift Beech bought Bianca led to both their downfalls. Beech lost her place of honor in the mansion and at table. Her Main Street dignity toppled too. A child thrashed halfdead upstairs. The mansion and its staff stayed unmusical and overlit in penance. Everything was said in harsh un-Psalmish English. Doctors refused to even let old Nurse go near the little victim.

They idly blamed Beech without quite saying so. Twice they'd found her sleeping on the hall-floor outside the sick room — her head resting on the huge black book.

Next dawn, Mr. and Mr. McCloud heard Maimie arrive for work that early. She had banished herself to the backyard. She'd asked to spend the night in the gazebo. She was denied permission. What first sounded like a mourning-dove reunion proved to be Miss Maimie's endless scripture-quoting vigil. Angus rose, looked out. A fat Bible rested open across Beech's long bone thighs. Her black finger speeded so, it tore one page's precious tissue. She pressed it back, apologizing to the Book, mashing the tear like it might heal. Beech, her prim hat knocked off-center, sat hunched on a lawn bench whose castiron made it look formed all of ferns — petrified ferns wanting more than anything to serve one person as group-effort fern-furniture.

From the upstairs window, Angus listened at chanted Old Testament lamentations — ones so suitable for awful troubles and, therefore, child, too often far too suitable for you and me. (Might be one reason The Book is the second best-seller of all time. Behind the Sears and Roebuck catalogue. A fact. Look it up.)

McCloud came lordly down the stairs. Cook still slept. In his tasseled robe, Angus personally made tea for Maimie. (A newly-rich Jack-of-All-Trades, he loved mornings best — each one seemed born with a message printed on its lower-left border: *Imagine your name in this space.* Angus' pride was worldwide shop-talk plus knowing how to do most everybody's chore just a bit better.) Of his efficient household staff's two dozen souls — he'd only felt awe at Maimie's mischief-squashing talent. Now, she too had proved mortal, disappointing. — Why was Angus always surprised when another minor wizard slipped? It hurt him every time.

Wearing just his robe, he carried out a tea tray, and one warmed scone. Beech blurted what she'd had all night to prepare: That day it'd happened? she'd only blinked after reading the Good News too long in a row. Her baby slipped right off. *"Now* look what's gone and grabbed her. Lord bound to punish Maimie. Unh huh. 'Eye for eye.' Exodus 21:24, Leviticus 24:20, Deuteronomy 19:21, Matthew 5:38. 'Eye for eye.' You watch."

"We must neverr talk like that," Angus said. He explained he wanted Beech to eat and drink while he could see her. She'd lost weight she couldn't spare. His indigo-blue robe's hem was wet with dew. He pulled satin around his red-haired legs, settled beside Maimie. Both folks could hear the household waking. They could see three daughters' heads peek out. Servants soon studied this odd pair resting side by side in a green backyard as green as greenbacks.

Angus said he remembered how, like him, Maimie was a orphan. He said he understood how this made such family as a person finally found (and founded) mean all the more to that person, did it not? "That person . . . ," she began but nodded instead, "person . . . so sorry." Her hands kept opening and closing her Bible, its cover flexed the way a perched butterfly will cure its wings in sunlight. Angus, watching, understood she hardly noticed. He reached over and—with a tender manly touch—stopped her. "Oh," Beech said, ashamed.

Angus shifted more her way. In full daylight, she looked so refined and yet—blinking—Beech seemed mystified at where her power'd gone. McCloud regretted that her secret weapon must now stay a secret—unpatented. He once imagined having Maimie dictate a book's worth of How-to's at one of his secretaries. Since the accident, Miss Beech looked so stranded— wings clipped, a poor buzzard forced to hobble forever along the ground. McCloud asked that Beech please go home today, just rest. He swore he'd send word if their wee child's health changed, either way.

"Our wee child," his ripe baritone allowed itself the sloppy luxury of repeating. In him, words' sweetness released a wallop so dark and syrupy it became almost a poison. The big man let hisself again feel what losing poor Bianca'd mean. The last time Angus indulged this, he'd raged around the homeplace tearing down stifling drapes.

Now, not even planning to, he reached out, took up this old woman's black bone-rake of a hand. He squeezed it, saying, "*We* underrstood her." Maimie only nodded. Angus saw her face split, pod-like. Weeping, her wrinkles softened from the deepest center-creases outward. Each of Maimie's braids, tipped with rag, seemed worn to blot one tear.

These two people—holding hands—soon felt semi-embarrassed, child—but not enough to stop. Angus, consoled by Maimie's touch, saw fit to cry in a steadied determined way. Tears, leaving him, seemed Grief's most natural dividend. Beech sat still, swallowing hard, admiring his ease, fighting back her own strange need to scream, to fall against him, begging, blaming. Fifty nine years of doing good. Now this. No credit. A person got no credit. Her account was all Checking. No Savings. Nothing saved.

Maimie waited to know what emotion—if any—would be possible here with everybody looking. Angus' solemn gulps sounded so much like his baby-daughter's. Beech had comforted hundreds of crying white children but never a grown white boss, and surely not whilst holding that gent's pink cabbage-rose of a hand.

She knew that under his slippery Bible-days robe, Angus must be naked as a boychild. This held no mystery or charm for her. Just made her feel the sadder for them both and for

Bianca upstairs.

Needing to sob aloud, Beech tried not to (a knot of push and pull). The shoulders shook—her fingers moved in short accidental jerks—and Angus' hand, scaring her, returned the pressure—his usual 'Let's do *this* now' authority.

Soon these two practically Indian-wrestled, strength matching strength. They almost hurt each other and respected doing this. They found it someway helped. Neighbors, servants and children watched amazed from many windows.

Down there, Angus quaked, bucking, steadily moaning, 'Oh Lard God.' Unashamed, he coughed and shook so. Out sounds came. Stripes of salt-water ran clean down his smooth ruddy face. He hadn't shaved yet but pinkish stubble didn't check the tears. Soon his wet chest and belly shone. A pint of water cooled his butterscotch skin, Angus quieted some. "Well," he said, wiping cheek-bones with the back of one free freckled hand. "Well well." Tears had darkened his indigo lapels to black.

Maimie's wrinkled brown face could've been a mosaic made of wild rice. She hardly let herself breathe now, elbows punishing ribs. If she blurted even one raw sound, it might explode, might prove more shaming than breaking-wind beside the Governor during some long mixed-doubles seesaw Psalm of French. Don't.

Angus McCloud had profited from crying a pint. He sat here steaming, spent like some lover cleansed sleek. Maimie'd released two crooked thimblefuls of tears. But this wetness kept so busied, was so mazed inside her face's crevices and folds, the woman's starchy collar stayed bone-dry.

Hands still gripped but less hard, each too polite to break the other's hold. Neither person dared look toward the sickroom, the only second-story window still bandaged behind velvet draperies.

From adjacent homes and many household windows, people

in pajamas stared down.

Sunlight found this fern-bench, a man and woman seated here, facing dead-ahead, stiff as any King and Queen park-statue. It was already getting hot. All over town, rough-sounding local roosters crowed.

Straight-up.

The earth is the Lord's and the fulness thereof. Roosters called direct toward sky. To Beech, their cries sounded like a homemade Psalm she'd chanted down down at fifty nine years of fussy-eaters:

"Be nice. Open up. It's me."

But I wander. What had to happen has to happen—even in the story of it later, child.

The accident itself. With personal money from her taming-Bianca bonus, Maimie L. Beech, 68, bought her dear child, newly 5, a birthday gift: some grown-lady perfume. The price of the bottle has been lost to us but we know it came from Woolworth's and was very very sweet—even for a humid magnoliaed backyard during three-pianos'-practice in green Falls, mid-May. Too much sweetness can become dishonest and a poison. Remember that. (And, child—I'm just guessing here, but—do you figure too much poison might reverse itself? Couldn't *poison* come full-cycle and swing back to sweetness? —For our clogged spoilt World, I dearly hope so. We deserve it. We deserve better.)

It's the day after a party for fifty handpicked children, Bianca's brown cigar-curls need yet another washing. Maimie carries one edgy child into the backyard, she places Bianca on two dozen thirsty towels. The girl feels tired from behaving right-well

during her party. A few lapses: she pinned-the-donkey-tail onto/
into two bossy visiting mothers. Then she purposely broke her
sisters' gift, a brown celluloid hat-pin box ("It's *ug*-ly, it's too
old for me, I hate it.")

In such pre-hair-blower-times, damp-headed ladies enjoyed
setting outdoors in direct sun. Just take along your brush, a
novel, a talkative friend or all three. Nice ritual—one now lost
to us, as is the wholesome scent of clothes dried by a passerby
Spring breeze.

Bianca—deeply trusting somebody for the first time in her
five jumping-bean years—lets herself now be arranged face-up,
formal as the corpse of some exceptional Egyptian princess.
Glad to finally be recognized as shy, she closes her blue eyes—
eyes so richly lashed they're awninged. Maimie counts the curls
aloud—Bianca's hairdo averages between forty nine and fifty
one, depending on humidity and whim. Beech tugs out each
curl so it's at its fullest length sunning along terrycloth. I picture
all of this (and Momma) from above. Feels like I'm in air
or else wellhid up the loftiest of McCloud pecan trees. From
Bianca's head down there on white towels overlapped in grass—
damp curls spoke everywhichaway—they shoot like rays from
off some spongy young sun in training.

Maimie occupies a ferny yardchair—The Bible rests against
her like the next infant she'll tend when reading spoils this
present darling. Looking over at Bianca, the old woman feels so
gladdened. Many casework-kids in turn have seemed Maimie's
favorites, but especially this one. It pleases Beech, reviewing
simple secret weapons: Never talk 'down' to your baby. Treat
yours the way *you'd* expect to be treated—which means loving,
hard. Love is a secret weapon, a serious profession and not—
(like for these uphill parents)—some fond sideline hobby.

Bianca has steadily begged to attend Beech's Wednesday

Night Prayer Meeting. Earlier this week two wary parents
finally agreed, "Only because you've been verra good, only
owing to our implicitly trusting your Beech here so." Parents
later worried that a child's getting so Good might mean her
getting a bad dose of that Old-Time Religion. Privately they
said, "First we'll get her civil. Then we'll discourage the rest."
At Afro Gethesemane Baptist, Bianca arrived in state. She
allowed Maimie's five favorite Sisters to come out of the choir
and make much over a stiff white dress, white hat and shoes.
On request, she said ten things in French ("Pass the butter, if
you please, dear dear Maimie of mine.") She apologized for a
accent that her big sisters swore was perfectly shameful. Bianca
soon went forward and got saved. Just like that. Outloud the
girl admitted how bad she'd acted, said she regretted putting
poor Maimie back there on the sixth-row through pretty-much
total-hoops but promised she wouldn't ever be that again, bad—
if possible. Then she looked around and begged to be dunked.
"Not while you wearing that, you don't," Nurse called aloud
whilst beaming. Everybody laughed. Bianca didn't feel taken
real serious here.

    She'd believed that Baptising-water would—under your feet
—go thick, instantly lidded like chocolate pudding's leatherish
cap. Water would support the walking weight of a saved little
girl. Imagine hiking over any wet you liked, be it bathtub, be
it flood. Your sisters would just hate you, they'd feel sorry as
they sank and drowned like Pharoah's troops. Bianca pleaded
now for Baptism, swearing that *Her* Jesus would keep *Her* outfit
dry, she knew He would. Bianca announced, "My Jesus will
be Water-wings." She sounded sure as her Poppa sounded at
his surest, darling, which was sure. This deeply impressed the
entire congregation. Amens sprouted row to row. Older ladies
rolled eyes, shook heads, sighed, "Tell it." Friends had *heard*

their Maimie Beech brag on this most recent child, now sure enough.

And: Here in present sunshine, Maimie, remembering all this, feels so pleased with a girl's Christian progress, feels so exceptionally appreciated at this address—she trots inside the mansion, fetches back the birthday perfume. Beech kneels on towels. (Maybe she should ask Mr. Angus hisself for reading-lessons? 'Go to a busy fellow if you want things done.' —If Beech finally admits her lacks, can she finally rest? rest here?)

Maimie douses her favorite's every fat sleepy curl. The dime-store calls its best perfume *Instant of Joy.* Out flows all that amber liquor. "Noint/you/sweet/head/Maimie oil/Cup/runneth/over . . . goodness/mercy/ dwell/ house/ Lord/ ever/ 'men/."

Her baby will soon wake in a cloud of sweetness bought with Maimie money. It'll be a surprise—like your coming-to in a tailormade halo all yours. This smell—addressing the earth's mysteries, feeling on a first-name basis with earth's fulness—this smell will say, "Open up. It's me." Kneeling, Beech closes her own eyes. Scent lifts a choir of chemicals amens.

Sunlight only swells the scent. It grows close to a sound like Psalms' own trumpets. Scent competes with upstairs pianism of a right high order. —Sweetness sends Bianca pegs deeper into honeycomb sleep. A six-hand arrangement of one Schubert song reaches her. Maimie adjourns to a Bible waiting—warm as life—on sunning castiron ferns. She opens to Psalms, shuts her eyes tight, sniffs her own excellent-smelling fingertips, dozes.

The good lunch was heavy, the good sun feels hot. Four black helpers are assigned to tend each white-one in this hive of mansion. A McCloud future is based on the Poppa's sought-after secret-formula: the most convincing available Blue. Every-

thing in sight seems certified: the verra best. Life comes with
a warantee.

The accident is gathering, unnoticed.

Maimie, nodding, dreams dreams. Swans are on a bright
river—upper bodies white and easy-seeming, hidden colored-
rubber feet are paddling hard to read the currents—and suddenly it's Jesus alive in person astride one row boat—His is a
Scotsman's pink-orange beard. He leaves the boat to walk, He's
wearing a manly white bathrobe so starched it's caulked solid
as a upright bouy, pretty as a good girl's crinoline. His pockets
are leaking bits of gold. Coins fall straight-down through deep
water He's exempt from and just strolls.
I'm mostly guessing here.

Fact: my Baby Momma wakes. Where? Oh, out in sun, on
shampoo day, must be birthday-perfume so strong everywhere
like evaporating shellack or doctor's office, —music, sisters . . .
Oh, okay, Home . . . But a new sound seems the one fact out
of place. (A drone, snipping, clicks like from castanets being
demonstrated downtown in the Courthouse Square six blocks
off.) Any person peeking from a pecan tree overhead would
notice one change: Bianca's pale brown hair should've dried a
fairer color than when wet, but it's gone darker. See, two or
three hundred black wasps have been drawn to this maybe-
overly-literal Woolworth's perfume. Gathered bugs now fret and
fidget, sucking at the sweetness sogged along each outspread
curl, roads all leading to one Rome, the soft white head of a
child who don't even know yet. She's been behaving lately, so

why *is* this?

Bianca's hair fans out around her. Her feet are bare, she's dressed only in clean batiste panties and a pretty little satin shift. Bianca sits forward, scared to look behind her. Something's about to happen just in back of her. She knows this. Bianca's head feels covered with a new weight, shawl or helmet. War bonnet. The sleepy child, curious, now touches the back of her own skull—mashes twenty jet-black stingers into pale scalp.

Here the scream should come. Here fur on the neighbor's cat should lift, all pianos hush, Maimie jump, and everyone like mad come running. But in Bianca's mouth's—complaint, warning, fury—can't, quite, move, through, teeth clamped this tight owing to a kind of pain she's never known before or even guessed at. Till now, what's been amusing? the fires you set, seeing animals try and get away in time, grown people's ugly faces when they find out what you've done now. Those, plus Poppa always, and dear Maimie lately.

But how can anybody this spoiled and five be prepared for a first grief and so close-in?

She's quiet, owing to a tongue that suddenly feels swollen to the size of a dead trout some days dead. Poison makes the backs of Bianca's blue eyes spot with blackness then go wider awake. Her mind shoots everywhere—a new emergency of chemicals and thoughts, smeared.

Bianca—dainty, gingerly—hops up. She scampers, barefoot, off the towels and onto grass. Silent, graceful, she hurries. She wears pretty white underthings and the three glossy pounds of black. Bugs' humming means they're starting-to-be-upset. The child runs in seven hushed and urgent circles all around around one chair. It contains Miss Maimie Beech snoozing, mouth open toward her Bible. The child runs so light, she could be flying, winged herself.

The child's logic is poisoned, plus it was a child's to start with.

Logic tells her: Get down to the River Tar and drown them, baptise them into being nicer to you, you. —Logic tells her if she moves quick enough they'll blow off her like gnats do at a gallop. Meanwhile, hurrying, she makes some other mistakes: one being—hitting herself many times across the head and temples, ears, the neck. A cloud of black is out ahead of her, right into that she runs.

Through a rear gardengate, down cinder alley, soft barefeet go. She sacrifices shade. She leaves the safety of her sisters' doing rounded guardian Schubert. Bianca, soundless, somehow gets six blocks, seven. Courthouse Square is baking, totally deserted at siesta hour. She runs around the whole downtown alone.

Fat Mrs. Lucas of Lucas' All Round Store sits eating cheese. It got marked down today but is not moving. Nothing-doing here at 2 PM—except just now—fast as one of them squiggle-shrimps of bloodshot-ghosts that flit across your eyesight when you're looking from a shady place into a brilliant one—past the front door of this dim emporium—Mrs. Lucas spies a child dart by so-quick so-white in sun it seems a spirit. The body-part looks snowy, bare. The head smoked blind—busied with darkest-thoughts seeped out into a cloud, a mask and hat.

This black/white ghost lasts just a fraction-second. Mrs. Lucas' jaw hardly misses one chewing-beat of cheese-eating. And yet this goodsized woman, even whilst doubting her eyes, decides to act. Something decides *her.* (And God bless the lady for making my life possible by saving poor Momma's.) Mrs. Lucas' mouth plugged with discount-cheese she is trying hard to swallow, the mother of eight herself, is now in air, is off her stool—

goes up like the least-likely rocket ever launched. She's been shot vertical by the sudden panting strength Disasters can bring out in certain people—especially usually-fairly-slow parents secretly packed with just such save-our-babies surplus. She is no longer a fat red woman bored betwixt customers. She is a blurry flour-white angel, she's Diana in fast-motion. Whipping off her apron, she runs on tiptoe.

Barging out the door she leaves a cashregister and every all-round item totally unguarded. She is seeing she was right, it's real, it's spastic, roughly thirty feet beyond her. Mrs. L. is half-past the store's sidewalk tool-display marked "It's May. Think of your Neighbors. Get Your Yard Right This Year." She grabs a pair of hedge-clippers—not sure why till later.

What has changed this often-lazy woman into such a jump-back Savior? Something called 'You must'. It can make heroes of us in one second. It can just-as-easy show how deeply cowardly we are, can leave us knowing that forever. Which hurts. But her? Hey—she's running—it's the longest such trek she's made in twenty seven years since—during a church picnic—she ran unsuccessfully-on-purpose from the huge and horny Luke Lucas, then eighteen. She is now flapping her apron all around her like some bullfighter's cape, clippers are hid beneath. Mrs. L. chases a child she recognizes from behind as a definite McCloud, the wild youngest one that stole so bad till right here recent.

Nearing Courthouse Square, Mrs. Lucas—(made a temporary genius by adrenaline that will—in a short time—fail her the way genius fails some people early—a woman blessed with sudden-juice that'll leave both thighs chafed, her body taxed from two years' effort spent in six good goddess minutes)—Mrs. Lucas draws alongside one fast little barefoot child. The child is galloping with eyes closed, hands wavering in front of her like a drowner's underwater. Mrs. L. sees: the child's head is already

twice a child's headsize owing to what's released by shiny stingers
stinging yet. And the woman throws her apron over this entire
buzzing noggin. She uses her own running bulk to knock the
youngster off its legs and onto grass beside our War Memorial.
The girl goes into a cartwheel that looks almost planned. Mrs.
Lucas is seriously falling too, one prolonged respectful thud.
A girl's worked-on head is now resting in a woman's lap.

The perfume that Mrs. Lucas suddenly inhales is so strong
and unexpected, it almost makes that marked-down cheese come
up. She shouts at the slit-eyed features because they seem so
far away. She bellows past bugs curtaining a blue-white face.
—She does what you are always told in First Aid Classes:
'Remember to assure your victim aloud'. It's something that—in
being victimized by the victim of the *sight* of your victim—you
can easily forget. —A fine stout voice cries, "I'm here. It's Doris
Lucas, honey. It's okay. I know just what to do."

Like all of us, this lady during lunch-hour is really only
inventing it as she goes, child. She's horrified all-during. Sometimes you act because you're less scared of making a mistake
than of *not* making one in time.

Quick here: *fake* it.

Her own palms are being bitten so, stingers pock each hand
with little maplights. Mrs. L—hedge-clippers in one fist, chops
off long curls, throws brittle clotted curls as far as away as
possible. She's staring down into the open mouth of the poor
head she's pruning. She swats and crushes insects in the air but
never on the flesh itself. And even as wasps bite Doris Lucas,
she keeps yelling kind words down at what might be a corpse
by now, "Almost over, nearly done now, hold on, sug. They're
off you mostly. You're with *me*, it's Doris. Lucas. Doris's got

you. Fine, we're going to be fine here. We're almost through. It's over with, I swear to you, we're done. Breathe, you, *breathe.* For Doris, do."

And she pounds a child's back, pounds, pounds it.

At home: Schubert continuous, Jesus wades in dreams.

As for personal-property during such valor—the Collier twins arrive at Lucas' to buy rick-a-rack for edging a round felt table-cloth. Finding the All-Round Store empty of every last Lucas for the first time in human memory, these ladies choose to stand guard and are actually sweeping up already. Tending the counter, they're acting like this is their usual shift—Doc Collier's twins who've never had to sweep their own place, are really loving playing-store. They even sell a little marked-down cheese to a goodlooking colored fellow in from Apex. They even offer to wrap it.

A shorn head is finally opening to sun, free of hair, a child-mouth, breathing at last, allows a scream to fountain out of it. Scream cuts past and over the fat woman whose own breath stops dead. Bianca is a siren that stills the action of eleven hundred souls—napping, love-making, piano-playing, store-minding. First: the scream brings Maimie L. Beech out of sleep and onto her shoes and into the act of running—Bible held against her chest like a shield for discouraging bullets. She is bound the six blocks toward the sound, she feels capable of going head-first down into the troubled mouth of her beloved Bianca. All this before Maimie even understands why she's moving and to what and who she is and how she is not Jesus on some pond-promenade but one employee, mortal—before she knows what her beloved job is, was, and why she has just lost it.

To make a long story less gory and more short, the swelling
finally commenced to shrink after three weeks of what sickroom-
lingo still calls "touch and go." Puffiness slacked, but not before
it'd made a independent gargoyle-type beast out of the head of
one small girl. Bianca's face had widened to the width—gossips
said with their genius for citing things' dread sizes—of a bee
hive—"face spread that broad till skin actually tore from the
insides of either eye, or so one hears." Bianca's hands—from
trying to save the head—were near as swollen as the head.

Downstairs, wellwishers arrived each afternoon and evening. They spoke in low voices, many wore black. Mrs. Doris
Lucas herself turned up, rouged, fists bandaged, saying, "Anybody would've. Lucky to've *been* there, really," a heroine. The
cook had given word that no more donated casseroles would
be allowed into *her* kitchen. "They think I don't know my job?"

In the parlor, instead of lying, offering the usual story-
improvements granted Falls' sick and perishing—folks told true
tales. About the languishing Bianca, they recalled her spunk. No
angel, her. They skipped all recent advances Maimie'd brought
about. They told of serious former naughtiness. Vandalism, they
called Hijinx. Arson they named Playing with matches. The
quiet elder sisters, longing for keyboards—secretly mourned
their young Mozart and Schubert along with the family Baby.
Sisters now heard of fresh Bianca-crimes. Confused, they risked
minor-key smiles. News: several occupied-privies suddenly in
flame—cats granted hairdos, dogs found tied in human clothes.
The time Bianca sat on the brandnew maroon-velvet church
pew-cushion and smiled a strange smile and said, "P.U.," and
you know she had peed on and deeply *into* it. Why? Shyness?
You ever try removing pumpkin meat (and later its smell) from

seven hundred piano wires? Well, don't if you can help it. — Folks today made her brattiness a litany. Their stories of her brilliant no-no's tried to pull Bianca back from dimness. Folks wished *they* had been way worse when young.

"Nice" seemed counties closer to Dead than "Bad" was.

When Baby Bianca finally opened her blue eyes, everybody rejoiced. Maimie most especially. (If prayers were books, Maimie would've been through every library of the Western World since her child got stung.) Afro Gethsemane Baptist had steadily petitioned for the life of its recent saucy visitor. True, that girl had lived, but she'd brought bad stuff out of her three week nightmare in the dark. Maybe she confused the color of her coma or the black of wasps with skin-tones of poor Maimie Beech. When that loving fuddled nurse finally got squired up- stairs for a first viewing—when she stood in the open door, ashamed, hopeful, grinning, holding out a scentless bouquet bought with her own money—the child took one long look. The child swallowed hard then went straight up over the back of her carved bed, clawing wallpaper, trying to get away. The girl, covering her puff-pastry eyes with puff-pastry hands, screamed a scream that again cost people three heartbeats apiece for blocks around. Even birdsong lost its place. "Black!", is what Bianca shrieked. *"Black!"*, was the first word of her scared new life.

Poor Maimie's one mistake had been dozing off whilst hired to guard. The white girl blamed a black nurse for that—and through it, child—for all the pain on earth. No fair. But Wee Bianca felt it was this simple and this fixed. Angus McCloud gave Maimie L. Beech a large chunk of severance pay. He handwrote five pages concerning her sterling character (a letter

Maimie carried home stuck in her Bible and later learned, with
help, was maybe her all-time best). So then—nicely taken care
of—she sat in her small clean house by the river and slowly
understood she had been fired, if verra genteely. Since her livelihood had forever been tending rich white troublesome children,
since news traveled for as far as she could walk to work, her
single nap had cost Maimie L. Beech a good deal. She could
afford to retire but—without work—she had no baby of the
moment. Without that, what use in wearing starched whites, in
staying up to iron? Alone at home, there was no need to fake
daily Bible reading. This made the Secret Weapon feel less
worthy. *She* knew she couldn't read. God, all-knowing all-sight-
reading, surely knew. Still, Maimie missed going through the
motions.

So much of the grandeur in our lives comes, strangely, from
certain loving daily habits. "Here I am, doing *this* again.
—Amen." Yeah, grandeur. In a second, I'll explain her chancy
later life.

—I now want to mention how the "L." in Maimie L.'s name
stood for Lucille. Odd, that young Bianca—not remembering
just *where* she'd learned to love that name so much—later came
to call me, her only child, after the sad nanny she'd got fired.
—Another story.

Little Bianca McCloud, now age 5 going on 40, no longer
needed a zoo-keeper. Before the accident, fear meant nothing
to her except a nice taste in her mouth. Like Poppa's secret
blue, she manufactured it. Fear trailed her everywhere, a wake
of knee-high calamity. Cats scattered. Neighbors shut the lids
of their spinets and, for good measure, sat on the shut lids. Now
it had her. Fear did.

People change. Even children do. Especially kids. Catch
them young enough, you can twist a poor baby to most any

bentwood shape you choose. To make a violin, you wet the
wood and *hold* it there till dry. — What did a five year old believe
about her perfume/accident? Maybe she thought it was a punish-
ment for all her early mischief? Did she see it as the dark race's
revenge on white folks' strutting — all blackly visited upon young
spongy her? Considering this version, (a child's, fairy-tale
simple, fairy-tale wicked) I reckon it's no surprise: Bianca never
again exactly cottoned to residents of Baby Africa. That'd be
putting it mild, honey.

She'd no longer go downtown on Saturdays when the Courthouse Square was most swarmingly 'mixed' — sixty-some-percent
colored. If a big black dog ran across the McCloud lawn, the
little girl stiffened with something like shock. Her body temperature dropped and Angus had to rush her in the house, rubbing
at her pink toes and fingers.

After the accident, whilst Bianca convalesced in bed, her
sisters — working shifts — did whatever the un-brat asked. They
taught her to read. Her early favorites? How-To Books on
Manners. She soon demanded that her plain upstairs-nursery
be re-covered in the very best of polished chintz — but only
patterned in flowers — no birds or butterflies and certainly no
bees. She said *she* wanted a Steinway concert grand, and signed,
and did they come in white? She was soon scolding her big
sisters for their wallflower ways, pasty complexions, hours spent
practicing in shaded rooms, their murksome dowdy clothes and
social panic. Bianca had once speared her way through a neighbor's populated goldfish pond while farmers in a wagon parked
on Summit watched. Now, head shaved wholly bald, (that way
it'd grow out even and not clumpy) she observed high tea at
age five. For Bianca, everything had to be just so.

Before the perfume, her Poppa'd secretly loved paying off
complainers, the grumblers who brought in items she'd broke

or accidentally set afire. For Angus—the former up-and-coming cabin boy from Glasgow, a man who had his tartans-vests and kilts made only of 'hunting' plaids not 'dress' ones—Baby Bianca's every shredded frock once seemed some flag of victory. 'Just like me,'

a parent's fondest prayer, a parent's worst fear.

—Now he mourned his wild child's passing. (Secretly, he felt his son had died. He hadn't known he *had* one till that imp got stung out of this world, drowned in a blackness Angus felt to be as cold as the North Sea around 3 AM on a off-night midwinter.) The Indigo Baron now noticed: His Bianca was just a girl, just like the others, was she not? He missed being the weest bit afraid of her, that was it.

It's how the truly strong recognize each other. "Uh oh" turns to "Ah." Fear can be the start of truest love.

Having changed into a hedge that clips itself, Bianca Mc-Cloud later tried teaching her own rude Baby Lucille such personal topiary. With me, darling, it didn't really take. Back of Momma's misshaped character stood what she considered one oversight made by one servant, black. And Momma never tired of blaming. A terrible destiny—To think: *Others did it to you.* To know them others' color, to live in a hamlet whose citizens are 65% that shade.

Adult, Mrs. Bianca oftimes criticized our neighbors' gardeners and maids as 'exceedingly insolent.' She claimed that the verra rarest commodity on earth was something called: good help. Momma swore she wouldn't trust black servants far as she could throw them.

Alone amongst the white ladies of Summit Avenue's better end, she did her own housework. It just embarrassed everybody. Me too. Others' maids—bound for work—clucked, saddened to see so finely-made a white woman out washing her own

windows, hanging perilously off the side of our house, her head
wound in a ugly-making indigo-cotton-rag and sweating like
. . . a stuck pig, waving down to all and calling, "Hot day, nasty
job. Must be *done* though." And basically loving it, child.

She'd grown up in that showplace home based upon some
idea of order in Edinburgh. (Angus McCloud hisself hailed
from less-toney Glasgow, but stocked his place with huge oil
paintings of Edinburgh Castle, aiming in everything he did to
be Edinburgh fine-grained, Edinburgh-worthwhile). —Someway, knowing that Bianca McCloud Honicutt was *his* heiress
made our neighbors find her willful clumsy housework all the
sadder.

"Lucille, it's a race that does not *mean* to steal." (In 1900,
this view made my Momma a liberal by local standards.) "They
simply take a shine to something and, the next thing anybody
knows (themselves included) a person's signed Paul Revere silver
sugar bowl, my dear dead Poppa had one, is in their handbag
soon to be displayed on some pine mantelpiece ꞌdownhill. One
doesn't blame a magpie for hording certain bright items in its
nest. So, we mustn't blame *them*, is how I see it."

The earth is the Lord's and the fulness thereof.

—Poor Momma.

And, oh yeah, what of Maimie? What about my Bible-believing
namesake who—in her day—had made so many white children
'straighten up and fly right'? She could not get work. Not
anywhere. Six months and nothing. Once she was put in charge
of a promising new bedwetter but, second day she turned up,
news had struck. Beech was asked to leave at once, please.
Nothing *per*sonal. People now claimed she was just bad luck.
Sleeping on the job, they said. Luring harmful Nature to the

one whose nature she'd been hired to iron out.

Finally a committee of five black ladies from her church took a train then hired a wagon, arriving unannounced at the flagship Indigo plantation of Angus McCloud. High walls surrounded his Headquarters. Angus—with two Chemistry majors' summer help—had concocted the secret formula for making semi-colorfast indigo dye. Others wanted it. The trip costs Sisters a two-day-journey. Showed how much they meant it. Maimie's onetime employer recognized this, asked them to sit down, please.

"She ain't set foot in church since the day it happen," one woman started. "Which ain't *like* Maimie," one lady added. "We been worried sick," a third stated. "Over her," the first put in. They talked like this, such tagteam sentences. Though not related by blood, at Garden Gethsemane they called each other Sister and were. They'd belonged to one choir since childhood and now seemed to think and move the way they'd sung forever four times weekly: one harmonized and quietly-fiery unit.

The group let on as how Maimie sure pined to see her little girl again. Angus said that just won't possible. Doctors' orders: another scare could set Bianca off. Unfortunate but true.

"Maimie ain't *just* sad."

"She running out."

"Of cash-money."

These friends knew better. Maimie lived alone, she'd saved for life, she only spent on church-tithing and treats for her former-children. (Beech hand-delivered a gift on each's birthday. She carried presents in person, hoping to see how another year'd changed each lapsed child. This also spared Beech having to address the package, write a card. Maimie's first brats were nigh into their sixties now. "Well, look who's here," they'd say to a shy smile. "Like the proverbial elephant, never forgets, does she?")

During the long trip to the coast, Sisters decided: if they couldn't get Maimie rehired, if they couldn't get her back on visiting-terms at McClouds' mansion, they'd at least try squeezing more retirement funds from Person County's third richest man.

"Cash," that man now admitted, "might be forthcoming from me here of late, Lord be praised. Especially considering my family's feelings for Maimie. Verra devoot. Starling character. Ever so prompt. A genius with children, Beech was, is." He took out a checkbook big as a Bible. The Sisters noticed: twelve joined checks made up every page.

"Lord be praise," ladies answered, a solemn breasty sigh rolled forth. What'd made these women travel so far and act this bold? Maimie's absence from their midst. It felt killing. She used to move and breathe and speak with them like this. Downtown with her on Saturdays, Sisters grew flustered, pleased and troubled when fancy whitefolks, knowing Maimie from the McClouds' very dinner table, nodded, touched hat-brims, said without a whit of question in their voices, "Beech." They said it like you'd factually say "Day" or "Night" in greeting. Maimie took this as her due. Made the Sisters feel a bit more visible and Maimie-famous. Beech's memory for Scripture was much-admired at Church. Her absence from among oldest friends felt like a amputation.

She'd been the unit's single skinny one. Sisters loved carrying food to Beech's house, forcing her to eat it while they watched. She stayed their only unmarried member, the one unmother. —First they'd tried matching her up with their Bible-believing brothers and flashy brother-in-laws. But the men came back, sat down real hard, rubbing their tired eyes, whistling, "I already *finished* school. She only talk about some cute wicked rich white

twins uphill. Do *I* care? She din't notice me not all night long."
So be it, lady-friends decided—Maimie'd stay more truly theirs.
These five appreciated Beech's refined ideas—they loved her unlikely spying-news from the great homes. Mail-order bees!
Though two of these Sisters taught school, they felt like Maimie's
years uphill made her almost their educated equals—whether
she could technically read or not. Maimie had no family. These
friends were her age or younger but forever treated her as
something of pet, their secret child. Odd, Maimie let them. She
knew just how to sulk and give-way after years of white brats
practicing on *her*. To Sisters it now seemed their oldest dearest
child was fading quick. This made them fearless. They'd do
anything to revive a woman who could be prissy and had real
high standards but—if in the mood—might make low-down
grumbly jokes with the best of them.

"Does this seem fair?" McCloud had written a check for
eleven hundred dollars.

"Lord *be* praise."

He told ladies that their own food and carfare should come
out of this. He stood and thanked them for their trouble, for
being such good friends to Maimie L. Beech. Angus said he
personally missed her verra much but that it couldn't be helped
after what'd happened which was nobody's fault, was it? Who's
surprised that wasps are drawn to sweetness? So much awful-
ness in this world just cannot be blamed, can it? On hearing
this, four women cleared their throats. One friend held the blue
check, others grouped around. Soon one fingertip of each Sister
touched a part of it. The unit didn't seem disposed to leave
McCloud's office yet. A board meeting waited, mumbly, in the
ante-chamber.

Angus leaned back against his desk. He didn't say, "Ladies,
I am, I fear, quite a busy man, I fear . . ." Instead he grinned

his ginger grin, "This *has* been a fine visit. I believe you've got everything?" They then looked at him, they did so very hard and very neutral. The center-woman spoke alone (slowed by trying to become others' choir and quorum all her self). "This gone probably seem like a lot to Maimie. But she ain't herself no more."

"You feel my amount's insufficient?"

The speaker got nudged by four soft shoulders from behind. She shrugged then—but left her own blank-check of a look aimed Angus' way. He thanked the women, hard. A gent fitted to do well in this world—Angus chanced adding, "Lorrd be prraised?"

"Lord be praise," the unit sighed. And left.

Maimie's friends were headed home, not-unpleased, taking turns holding a blue chit. Their preacher was knocking at Miss Maimie's door. Smiling, the elderly gent explained: *he'd* found a way of easing Maimie's mind. God had whispered it to him after supper last night. Hat off, Rev. stepped in, uninvited. There were, he said, so many *black* children heareabouts who might could benefit from M. L. B.'s years of uphill practice. In Baby Africa, so many youngsters were flat-starved for Maimie's one-at-a-time kid-glove type care. Why didn't she cheer herself by tending *them*, us, ours? Beech's plaits had come unfastened and dangled like risky laces trailing a untied shoe. She'd lost weight you never knew she'd had. She looked more pure and vertical. Less a virgin, more a warrior.

"*God*", Beech said, "whispered you that? Free babysitting from *me*?"

She had not offered Preacher tea or even water. She stood, proving this'd be a short visit. On the table behind her, partly-wrapped presents: fifteen leather pen-wipes and twenty bath talcs. Hat bunched in hand, Pastor said: his job was delivering God's word. What folks then *did* with it was their business.

"Well, sir," Maimie rubbed her eyes like a reader burned steadily by the world's finer print. "One thing is, I real used to being *paid* for it. Got pretty good money uphill too. *You* should know—I been tithing right along, paying *you*." She explained she'd steadily worked for 'quality'. Maybe that'd ruined her, who knew? But these ragged weedy young-ones from down-around-here? well they just didn't rightly *mean* as much to Maimie, you know? Did that surprise him, had she gone and hurt his feelings? "Not to boast none," she went on wrapping gifts, "But I been called a genius at getting the Spoilt to do right. Could be, all my time *around* the Spoilt has done spoilt Maimie too. But, way I see it, if *I* can't cure me of my being ruint by spoilage, then can't nobody else. —As to my doing-for these little black ones? free of charge? noo, that don't really draw Maimie un*to* it all that much, sir, but thank you."

He turned to leave. "Sister," he tried a last time. "You know this, but . . . Charity begin at home." "Fine," Beech snapped. "Go start at *your* place. In this house, my remembered babies keep me steadily busy, sir. I believe they calling Maimie right now. Good day."

She saw him ease down her porch steps, the man looked caved-in, that disappointed with his old favorite who knew the best 100 from the Book of Psalms' 150. She grabbed up her Bible (dust was on it—troubling, the strange deadly feel of grit there). She ran to her porch, didn't even bother opening the Book but mashed one hand across its cover. Then—like receiving telegram-knocks—she quoted aloud at his bent hurrying back: "Preacher? We all 'discipline problems'. You too. Who is ever going to take us in Hand? Psalm 14 it say 'Lord looked down

from heaven upon the children of men, to see if there were any
that did understand and seek God. They *all* gone aside, they
are all together become filthy: there is none that doeth good,
no, not one.' — Everybody a brat underneath. Maimie ain't the
only one spoilt rotten." Three children were playing with a
wagon wheel on the dusty street. They went still, watching.
She'd once been this neighborhood's example. Mothers told brats,
"Get out that lazy-bed and come to this window, notice our
Sister Beech." There she strided, stern uphill in virgin-white,
Bible clutched against her, bound daily toward making children
of the grand do Godly. She now knew from streetkids' faces—in
her half-year out of work, she'd become a witch. Beech touched
her un-tended hair. This uniform seemed soiled. "You so ill-*bred*
to stare," she shook her Book at them. "You bad." — She hurried
indoors and leaned against the wall. It crackled with hundreds
of children's yellowing drawings.

How could she ever tell her preacher and Sisters what it
meant to eat alone, a meal without one living child nearby to
stroke and cleanse and stuff? Food interested her none at all
now—Maimie by herself hardly seemed worth cooking for. She
was accustomed to dining at the Governor's fancy table or else
lolling in a sunny nursery alongside her darling—or even sitting
at the Staff lunch, Bible opened before her so she wouldn't have
to talk to simple under-gardeners and such. Sent to her home
downhill, Beech first struggled to make one nice meal a day,
she'd tried amusing herself. She uselessly ironed her uniform at
night. All day, she wore the nurse's cap around her kitchen. She
told herself kiddie stories—the one about a king that turned
everything he touched into refined genteel gold—a king that
couldn't keep his mitts off of his favorite little girl—that made
her too be valuable, 24 carat and dead, dead.

Bored of food, (a rich person's ailment caught uphill) Beech used tricks perfected on five decades of fussy eaters. This woman alone at a table in a house, lifted a spoonful of hominy grits. She held it before her own resisting mouth. The mouth called sing-songy, "Knock knock? It's me. Open *up*, Maimie's Sweet Flower. Cause here come big fat old Mr. *Bumb*le Bee."

Then she heard herself. The woman alone at a table in a house, lightly set her spoon aside. She mashed both palms flat against wood. She stared ahead.

Five Sisters, returned to Baby Africa, brought McCloud's blue check direct to Maimie's home. She didn't look so good. Her face was ashy as she thanked them. "I hopes," she said, her back turned toward these dearest friends. "You didn't beg him for it or nothing. I right fixed, moneywise. It ain't the money so much. I hopes Mr. McCloud give it freewill-like."

"He seem real glad to." "He tell all kinds nice things on you." "We figure he got off mighty cheap." Maimie thanked them but cried again. They all prayed together, holding hands, hoping to regain their nice old working unit. Traveling ladies then dragged on home, exhausted. Wilmington's 'True Blue Unltd. Indigo Camps Inc.' was as far from Falls as many of them would ever go. Only on account of loving Maimie had these Sisters made the sacrifice of distance.

Toward their houses, women scattered to pray for Beech whilst bathing, steeping. (Water can be a form of prayer—a lightning-luring conductor even for the Spirit.) Tonight was Wednesday Night Bible meeting. Again Preacher would mention Maimie's health. For nearbout seven months, he'd kept her on the 'Favored Shut-in's Church-Pillar Prayer List.' Secretly, while praying under a flutter of Amens like pumping wingbeats, all of Afro Gethsemane set there, eyes closed, blaming blaming one white child.

Sisters back from duty found their home-porches alive with husbands unworthy or over-worthy. Their sinks were piled with days of dirty dishes. The backyards were littered and too loud with children less refined than their chosen mascot Maimie. But after *her* bare box of a house, a person did feel joy in greeting loved-ones' noise, the pleasure of this much friction waiting to welcome a body room-to-room. Just another soul's saying (without even being real-deeply interested), "So, how *was* it?" That helped. You compared your life to Maimie's choices — walls coated in baby-scrawlings, total silence, one big calendar Xed grand with big-wigs' birthdates. Maimie — and her kindergarten of white ghosts — ghosts that hadn't even held the door or waited for her. Ghosts that'd betrayed her — not staying baby-ones but growing up on her and coarsening, forgetting.

Maimie L. Beech, alone now, paced. She appeared to seriously read one upside-down piece of blue paper — (indigo-blue for purposes of advertising and as a little joke). To her, the amount seemed huge. Embarrassment ran just that size. Stashed with her own savings, this meant she'd have enough to live comfortably forever. Why did that now seem a endless jail-term? McCloud's gift felt rigged, each dollar had a stinger hid inside it. Money planned to slowly numb her, hush her, keep her calm downhill and minding rowdy children her own shade. Once Maimie turned McCloud's blue paper into hard yellow gold, she would sign away her last true claim. She tried and calm herself with scripture, "Psalm 90 go: If his children forsake my law, and walk not in my judgements, if they brook my statutes and keep not my commandments, then I will visit their transgressions with the rod and their iniquity with stripes." To the

blue check, Beech explained, "I been famous. Fa-mous." She
kept pacing.

'The Secret Weapon' they'd called her. This pay-off meant
Goodbye to remembered French at table, so-long the Book of
Palms. Bye even to the scary half-fun of smelling smoke, dashing
toward it, screaming, "Sugar, sug, what *now*?" Beech was being
asked to cash in her Bianca like a stack of soap smooth ivory
chips.

"No way," said Famous Maimie Beech. "No way in *this*
world." She walked back and forth, the check pulling nearer
her long face and weak eyes. She pictured what gold this paper'd
draw her at the bank. She imagined it: a head-sized pile of rattly
yellow light, coins that someway rhymned with all the thousand
gold/brown/yellow ringlets sprouting off pink babies all those
uphill years. Around her finger, she'd created them from fluff,
from nothing much—the definite and separate curls, proud years
of them. Baby ringlets seemed a type of coinage too—maybe
this earth's tenderest denomination. Rich folks—out all-day
earning still more money—had onct felt proud to leave the
costly Maimie Beech guarding their true treasures. Even as
a slavegirl decades back, Beech'd understood: The hellions—
her chosen specialty—were oftentimes their parents' best-loved.
Everybody considered that being bad—wild, willful—meant
both a sadness and a luxury. There was heat in badness. Beech
knew. The homes might change, the children might look different, but out of baby-blues and baby-browns one thing scoffed
at her. It made housecalls and so did Maimie Beech. "How you
hanging, Marse Satan?", she said with a silent nod. And He
snarled back, "*You* again?" They were old enemies. She was His
Laundress. He was her filthy livelihood.

Beech had once felt so in-charge when big spenders called
her in, tried bribing her to come and tame their lively worsts.

She felt she'd pulled a fast one all these years — *loving* the brats had been her trick — it was that simple, that cheap. (McCloud believed a person got what a person paid for. Beech now saw — a person surely did. And she wanted it back, fifty nine years worth. Might be a seller's market but she'd re-gather all of it she could afford.)

What'd Maimie done for six decades except peddle her life-time's worth to the highest bidder? Everybody got issued a certain amount of love, per household — even residents of Baby Africa found their rightful share. But Hers? oh she'd been real clever, she'd rushed uphill and squandered it on sets of thankless twins, she'd spread it — gilding-powder — over idle little clumps of strangers' babies. Her share went to end their fevers, to hush their stammers, it'd urged their first steps. She'd burned her share in reading kids the finest things a hired head could make up. Years of it — sunk into scoldings and Bible lessons, the changing of those million diapers, all the rubber sheets.

No gentleman caller ever returned to her home after visit number three — not even when local gossips hinted how much cash old Beech had squirreled away. To her, no gent ever buzzed, "Open up. It's me."

Pacing, Maimie wondered, Was she one bit better than the women who accepted white men into their houses for a fee? Name the difference between loving these men and loving these men's brats? — At least the other act was over-with lots quicker. Even if nobody quite meant it, that deed was at least *called* "Love." Wouldn't it have been a faster, more honest livelihood than her years of patience — this gallery of scribbles, a few bronzed baby tokens, her tended calendar of honored births, and for what? Her birthdate was now nine weeks gone. Who had honored her?

She'd been Whites' 'secret weapon.' Love had seemed her

secret weapon against them. Now she saw: Love had been their secret weapon—against her.

She studied his blue check. It was, she saw, a polite white un-invitation. Marse McCloud was taking back that time he'd held her hand.

—A genius with children—kept far from children—why, she ain't quite a genius no more. Mostly she has sunk to being a bleachish watered ghost. The bank is broke.

Maimie shut her Bible on the check. She tucked both underneath a pile of white hand-me-down dinner plates. But even from the far side of her room, a tongue of indigo showed. She dressed to go out, she chanted verses Bianca'd liked, "Enter into His gates with singing. King in his counting house, counting up his honey. Know ye that the Lord He is God. Queen down in she parlor, eating bread and money." Maimie pulled the check out, weighed it with the salt and pepper. These shakers: metal-plated baby-booties—fitted with clear glass-inserts. Beech fetched her own unopened bottle of perfume—just like one she'd given to a birthday-girl. 'Instant of Joy' had been Maimie's mirror-image gift to herself. She slipped into her best white governess outfit, one kept back in case she ever got offered work again. She pinned on her crispest cap. Beech stowed the perfume in one pocket, clutched her Bible big as a Welcome mat—hiked off to Wednesday Night Prayer Meeting. She was greeted with screams, welcomed like the Dead returned to life.

I've only heard this next part third-hand, fourth-hand. Still, especially if you're named for the person, you try and understand what went on in her head that evening. We know the Service ended around eleven. Sisters walked Beech home. They all kissed her good night. They kissed each other. Friends felt they'd saved

Maimie's life. They were grateful she'd allowed them the excellent, justly-famous sensation of doing right.

(Wrong-doing is exceptional too and maybe has more variety—
but right-doing's pleasure lasts longer. —Or so somebody-as-
old-as-me must tell herself, darling. Be patient.)

Maimie waited till her loved ones meandered home. She
already missed them. They'd always admitted envying her uphill
reputation, amazed at how whites had kowtowed. Friends forever acted kind to her but, in the end, they always left to join
their real families. Beech understood: if she got sick, they'd tend
her. If she died, they'd carry-on proper and noisy at her funeral.
But—even after years of kindness—Maimie knew what her
'Sisters' knew: For a whole lifetime, it just won't enough.

Maimie—richer now—figured maybe she should haul off
and hire a nurse and stranger (maybe even a white one). This
person would come and stay with Beech tonight. The lady, a
professional, would bring along her knitting or letter-writing
but she'd first tuck in Maimie's covers, she'd say, "I'll be right
here if you need anything," she'd say, "There there" or whatever
honey-tongued hired-comfort said.

The nurse wouldn't have to mean it. Fact is, her words'd
help Beech *more* for having nothing personal in them. For being
bought at the going white-rate, pricey.

First Beech embarrassed herself by hiking uphill to the
McCloud home. She guessed this was a humongous social-
mistake-in-the-making. She couldn't stop. Being 'bad' was suddenly of major interest to her. "*You* again," she muttered and
knew she was greeting Satan, Satan stationed on-duty in herself.
If Beech set her mind to being bad—considering the years of
observing little wicked geniuses—who might be better at it?

A party was underway. Chinese lanterns lit the trees. Lanterns drooped from a harem of palms dragged onto the porch. Every pastel lantern glowed with one squiggled Chinese letter. Maimie had learned: no McCloud could translate these. Each character looked like Beech's vision of Oriental-Bible-English. Each looked written by some ink-dipped wing in flight.

Folks packed and jammered all over the McCloud lawn. You heard clinking glass ladles against glass punchbowls filling glass cups—sounded like the Caucasians were made, mouth and hands, of glass. Maimie mingled easy enough at first. Two young women asked her to please go get them some extra napkins. When she looked hard their way, one said, "Sorry. We thought . . ."

Three pianos sounded from indoors. Music leaked through open windows with the candlelight. A gatecrasher moon looked on through treelimbs. The mansion's hundred points and edges showed black against a sunset. This sunset was the color of foreign rubies or the best local berry jams.

All-in-white, the second-gardener stood carving raw roast-beef on a banquet table dragged outdoors. The smell of food made Beech feel giddy. Seemed she hadn't eaten for the longest time. How many days made a week and what was her day off? The nearer she wandered to the church-like home, the weaker did her legs feel. Finally—bumped and milling among glazed white strangers—Beech sat down on the lawn. She had to. She'd been staggering.

Waiting here in dewy grass, Beech held more tight to her Bible. (People would see the Book and know her.) She touched her scalp, was the hat straight? Facing the three-story uphill home, its stained-glass burning from inside like with a fever, Beech spoke as at some choosy eater . . . "Open up. It's me."

She only wanted rest. She felt like she deserved to rest right here. To someday be buried in this pretty grass—a gravestone white as a saltlick. Soon Bianca would know Beech was here, Bianca would dash out holding tailormade clover-anklets, a five-strand clover-crown.

Guests—though busy admiring, addressing and fondly criticizing each other—did slowly notice the curious sight: a black woman wearing a white uniform—sitting in grass as if stationed here for some useful chore, to read 'fortunes' from her big black book, or to bodily plug the yard's worst geyser, or give guided tours of clover. Nested among the pretty opentoed shoes of white ladies, shiny summer-shoes of gents, the seated woman was careful to keep her long neck stretched in a way half-grand—her pleated face wide-open with a look of full entitlement.

Out-of-towners' fancy shoes first edged away from her. Then one pair of white-suede oxfords did come nosing nearer, "Might we be of service?", the shoes had a young white male voice helping them from high above. "You're feeling a tad whoozy, I take it. Well welcome to a fairly largish club. My friends were just asking what our Presbyterian Angus uses to spike this stuff. Certainly sneaks up on one. Not that you don't look perfectly at ease down there, but—listen, should you ever *care* to stand, I consider myself still steady enough—possible mistake of mine— to maybe assist a person. —Say, are you a nurse? We were just wondering. Couldn't help notice your tidy little hat. Young lady in my group, see the one? she was admiring it. —Look at her giggling. Definite drawback. Don't you hate it when they giggle, Nurse?" "Tell Marse Angus my name. He know me. I used to help around this place. Set right at the table. Tell him Maimie L. Beech back on the job. See what he say do."

Beech understood: McCloud must now be sent for. Her order had been given. She was glad. Enter into his presence with singing. Sound the gongs, burn incense, waste precious precious ointments. When the gates swung open, when Beech was asked to enter again, she would know what to say or chant. She felt she did not need to plan it now. Her favorite hymn was: *Something Always Sings*. Just trust, she told herself—she gave herself some credit.

But Beech was down here shaking. Her dark legs—little wider than the bones in them—poked straight before her, ending in great blockish white shoes. She wore flats to shorten the distance she had to bend toward her children. Now hugging the Book, she waited among other feet. Her face changed, mouth almost-gloating, mumbling, ready to greet the man. She sat stubbornly grinning at nothing—plainly eager to become more naughty. Beech was laboring at it.

The young white shoes went off to others ("Seems to actually *know* Angus") then both shoes moved to the house, climbed nine front steps, returned: a message.

Clumsily, one whole young man bent down into sight and breathed whiskey at her. Beech closed both eyes. She never expected to see a person lower toward her like a diver coming down to join her underwater. This was the first direct order Beech had ever sent McCloud: 'Hear my petition. Come out to me.' Where was the man?

"Angus insists you meet him on your backyard bench, on you-two's bench. You *do* know him, don't you? Boss told me to tell you, at all costs, 'Bleach must not be seen by the youngest', that little one who always wears the hats, their baby one . . . named . . ."

Eyes shut, Maimie hoarsely announced with great tired feeling, "Bianca."

"Very one, yes. Boss said, under no circumstances should you be seen by her. I hinted as how—maybe you'll object—you'd perhaps imbibed a drop. Not that *I* haven't. (But then I have due cause I still work for him.) And Boss goes, 'Bleach is not to be seen by Bianca. Bleach will know this herself, in whatever state.' He said you were devoot! But why 'Bleach'? — Anyway, my advise'd be you go and try him now in the backyard. — You know, Clara's right. Especially up close, this is quite a cunning little hat you've got. Clara might even want it. I think I'm going to go *ask* Clara." — Maimie Beech nodded, careful to keep eyes mashed closed. She started to unpin her cap but the voice walked off. Beech let her hat stay while repeating in a dulled locked tone, " 'Cannot be seen here.' 'Can not no longer be seen here' — He acting so rude. He *rude* to me."

She had asked for a moment's credit and right out front where folks could see a person get her due — prepare a tale/presence mine enemies. He had not come out to her. 'Open up', she'd asked. The household would not. — Few saw the minor spectacle. Through groves of ankles, cuffs, pale shoes, paste-buckles, one lean black woman in outsized whites, eyes mashed shut, clutching her bible, scrambled away on hands and knees. She slipped from the lantern-lit yard, was soon just white shoes scuddling out a hedge's hole, was lost to the safety of the darkness of the street.

At midnight Beech someway trekked into countryside, never more than six minutes from Falls' most urban-type center spot. At Meacham's farm and apiary, something happened. Versions of it change with whoever chooses to tell you. Some claim Beech tried drinking the perfume as poison. Most agree she drenched herself with scent. Next morning, footprints proved she'd walked back and forth before the hives, kicking a few. But bees, helpless day-workers, stay home at night.

The broken perfume bottle was found under one of three rope beehives that Famous Maimie Beech overturned. Seems she smeared herself with honey. Morning showed a hillside clotted with wax-comb and gritty syrup. Many trapped bees floated under amber, stuck in sweetness they'd spent lifetimes making.

Maimie Beech then marched herself to the river. Maybe bees were stinging her the way she wanted bees to. Maybe she was only sticky and perfumed, a mess, disappointed. The river seemed the one place a person could be safe. Maimie opened her Bible and placed it on a flat rock near the roadway. No name was written inside, just one X traced many times to make it clearer and more hers. But the volume was bigger than anybody else's hereabouts and would be recognized. Its center had been most-worn away, leaving Psalms a frilly cavity (the book betwixt the terrors visited on faithful Job and the bossy hope of Proverbs). I imagine Maimie smelling the river, sighing many Psalms aloud, practically chugging them. I see her noticing the moonlight wavering on water like some flaming path or giant tongue. I imagine her good shoes testing water's temperature. I hear Famous Maimie Beech saying to the river, to the night and world—"Open up. It's me."

She steps off a rock into our River Tar. Easy to picture her starched cap becoming a little folded-paper-looking sailboat, breezing away without her. Maybe she planned to briefly run over the water's moonlit top, maybe she settled for walking on the surface, only to discover that she couldn't stroll much of anywhere except along the mud-bottom, a bottom that dips to thirty-five-feet there by our town's namesake Falls.

The body didn't turn up for the longest time. Later rumors swore that when four scared shad-seeking white boys fished her out near a factory near Tarboro—she had traveled further from Falls proper than ever before during her lifetime. With sun's bleaching, with her soaking in the tannic acid from a shoe-polish

plant outside Tarboro, the bloat of her had been someway bleached. It made identifying all the harder.

Tarboro authorities announced finding a 'possible elderly Indian nurse.' Falls had sent the official missing-person-notice, but if you're a town Tarboro's size you don't absorb the expense of having a body crated up and put on the Atlantic Coastline spur-train till you know whose body it's been. The Sheriff looked for ways to learn this. Not by dental records since this particular person's dental work had just meant taking out the hurtingest tooth one at a time. Nothing was ever put back in (which is all that really helps you to identify—the gold and silver additions. Those, people keep track of).

Sheriff spied a cross-shaped brass locket round this neck so swollen that he had to break the chain to get it off. He opened the latch and pressed a pulp of wet paper inside, paper oozing water like a eye. Sheriff then set the locket near his office-woodstove all day. He found he could finally make out what each dried thing had been. Using a knife, he peeled off one layer at a time. In order, there were modern-type photos moving back toward daugherrotypes then tintypes: likenesses of thirty nine white children. Some grinned. Many looked forced to do so. From a mischievious-looking curly girl at the front, Sheriff worked backward. Then, against the locket's very metal, he saw a red sticker and, finally, some writing that looked promising as ID.

"Okay now," he took the locket to his cleanest office-window. He held it up, squinted hard then read aloud to sunlight:

"Woolworth's Special Value 29¢."

Sisters found the bankcheck on her table still un-Xed. Blue paper was weighed by bronze salt and pepper slippers. The loving choirmembers had already scanned every page of Maimie's sticky Bible, looking for some jotted clue. Friends plundered Maimie's house till they destroyed its true first order and couldn't get stuff back the way it'd been. Still, they kept seeking some explanation. Maimie had received McCloud's tribute money. She had returned to church. So why'd she gone and done this godless thing?

Maimie Lucille Beech's best friends kept patiently ransacking her shelf and counters, seeking a note. It would maybe accuse Angus McCloud, it'd maybe say he'd done some deed beyond unfair hiring/firing. Maybe he had 'touched' Maimie— What if something off-color had gone on? This seemed unlikely but the women wanted to see blame placed where it belonged. They felt ready to accept Maimie's word for who to accuse.

Sisters quit hunting long enough to sit around her kitchen table. They sat looking at the bronze booties, one filled with white salt, one black pepper. Who had these tiny shoes once fit? Some plump sixty year old grandpoppa uphill? It made them sick to wonder.

Sisters felt tired and cross—almost cross with Maimie. The harder they looked for her last message, the deeper they felt: She'd never exactly been *like* them. Maimie had believed. That'd forced her to do so foolish. She believed too much in Them uphill. She disappeared when Them uphill stopped seeing her. She considered their eyesight some Sun that can kill you by just looking away. —And ladies decided, Maimie'd partly valued the Sisters because, like her, they'd been so shamelessly interested in the ones uphill—in Power of such bright white voltage that it sometimes passed for love.

Maimie had once seemed these women's aging child. That

now made them group-mothers of a suicide. (If the hardest thing on earth is losing your own child—how much rougher—losing that child *to* that child? —Why?)

They rose again in grouchy unison. "Well," two said. Rubbing lower backs, they turned and hunted the note in places they'd already checked twice. (Sisters had their own reasons for sadness and the little daily rages. —But their friend's reasons interested and puzzled them. They wanted to give Maimie Beech a last fair chance at listing hers.)

Finally one lady snapped strong fingers, "She *couldn't*."

"Read nor write," somebody added.

"Which mean: no note," another explained. "No way she *could* tell us."

Then they all went home. They felt guilty but released into their safer crowded lives. —Afterwards, even as their needing one another grew way keener, the surviving Sisters would never again be quite so much a unit. At church, even while singing, they would look at one another, hard. They'd always known everything that loving friends can do for each other. Really, so much! But now these women knew what they *couldn't* do for each other. It made them afraid. They resisted this but: it made them almost afraid of each other.

One excellent final question can often run you: *The money that set so much motion, where'd those big bucks come from?*

Well, like I said: Cotton and 1851–88, a small but profitable shipping-line out of Wilmington. But mostly Indigo—one cash-crop that proved of shortlived value. The plant itself was suitable to marsh-growing conditions much like Rice favors. Indigo got named for first being used in India. Its dye made a violent if heavenly violet blue. One drawback: the tint tended to streak. It got replaced by quicker easier chemical-processes just after our story ends.

Since indigo's money-making days are gone forever (and even if they should come again) I want to now reveal my grand-dad Angus McCloud's unwritten-down but passed by-word-of-mouth secret recipe. If he knew I was telling this, the man would probably spin in his bronze casket. — Angus who lived such a long full life and ran for Governor twice and lost twice. Angus who gained enough gold so one day he turned around and saw it all behind and under him, who suddenly understood the value of his touch and soon got stiff and precious over it, and frozen. He panicked he would lose everything. He stopped finding ways of making, and turned to ways of keeping, and was lost. First he became a Republican and then moved beyond that till folks claimed he should've run for state office — not on the Republican ticket — but on the Royalist one. These things happen, even to the self-made, especially them. Child? Beware of using up your last forty years in being the curator of your first fifty. — *That* ain't getting ahead!

The chemicals you need I've never really laid eyes on or touched. Still, their names I know. My poor old magpie mind just works this way. So, here goes the family-money's secret finally in black-and-white:

Take one part powdered-indigo to two-parts ferrous sulphate, combine and stir. Steep with three parts of slaked-lime. Then, before allowing your brew to perk for the three needed days, add — finally — two hundred parts water.

At Maimie's funeral, most white McClouds and nineteen of their black staff arrived in a stately queue. Angus and his silent diplomatic wife were accustomed to doing the right thing. Locally they'd grown famous for it. Servants hadn't planned attending, they'd disliked Maimie's privateness, her scholar's airs. But one direct-order from Angus, and here they mostly were. A skeleton-crew had been left to mind the Mansion Mc-Cloud. Of course, young Bianca McCloud won't present at this particular burial.

Her three big sisters had offered to play suitable sixhand funeral pieces. Their Poppa even volunteered getting the three Steinway-grands downhill from Summit Ave. to Gethsemane Garden True Gospel Afro-Baptist here near the river. Preacher expressed certain whispered doubts about his old church floor's willingness to support that kind of show-off weight. And though he thanked the young ladies, Rev. did let hisself wonder aloud if *their* type of Europe Music would be sufficiently homey or fitting for the end of a person as Christian, local and unemployed as the late Miss Maimie Lucille Beech.

These quiet girls, denied permission after practicing two-days-straight, still felt determined to do something right for Beech. They hinted to Poppa: he might offer pallbearers use of the healthiest palm plants, might have greenery sent down to Garden True Gospel for the service. Maimie'd onct asked permission to come uphill and water all the Palms one Palm Sunday (her day off too). She seemed to like these plants for secret reasons all her own. Girls sometimes caught Beech standing under one's droopy overhang, green fronds throwing louvered shadows on her dried dark skin. Her eyes would be closed, loose braids poking like feathers through a leafy weave. Her thumb and finger might be joined to hold the tip-end of one branch that she tugged slightly. Seemed its fibers sent her coded

vibrations: news or poetry, the fulness thereof. So Angus said: Liked palms, did she? fine, sure: And after breakfast, he called aside his third-gardener, mentioned which wagon should be used. Angus said to deliver, say, the mansion's twelve top-plants and get them into the church and set-up well-before the service began, and to retrieve them at a decent longish interval after-wards—so black folks would remember just their being beauti-fully *present*, and not get confused by seeing them fetched back home too over-carefully, and so forth. Understood?

Parents had left their little Bianca uphill today, unsupervised upstairs. She'd never let them hire a replacement nurse. Bianca's hair was now growing out if somewhat darker. (Angus'd wanted to buy a wig for his invalid—one made of real human hair from Irish girls who arrive at the hair brokers every five years and let theirselves—whilst weeping, quiet, resigned—be practically scalped for the money. —It pleased a Scot to purchase Irish hair for his American daughter. But Bianca's mother, in the one thing she will say in our story, rose up during dinner, slammed her fist on the table, shouted how: a wig of stranger's hair would only further lure death and tempt fate. "My child will wear a wig over my dead body." And sat again, having stated this strange picture.)

Mr. and Mrs. McCloud felt like their Bianca had meant it: in asking to stay home and practice scales on her new piano. Starting so far behind her sisters, the girl was really struggling to catch up. You had to admire the hours she put in, even if she maybe lacked their natural gifts. Worried about leaving her, parents finally decided that, after all, the cook, groom and headgardener would be just downstairs if Bianca needed any-thing and called out for a snack or help.

Angus McCloud now listened to the white-robed church-choir clapping near Miss Maimie Beech's pine box. Its lid was mercifully shut. Borrowed palms swayed, trembling with music and the choir's pooled breath. A blue envelope stuffed with bills crackled inside Angus' breast-pocket. His check written to Maimie had never been returned for payment. He planned making a notable donation to her church. But Angus slowly recalled: Collections aren't taken during funerals.

Which was pretty silly—especially with *him* present. Angus sat staring down into one of his rosy hand's opening and closing. A fly kept buzzing in the windowsill nearby. Angus imagined profits that would've gathered by now to the importer of that first bee-hive from Holland in 1602. Imagine if the guy could've just kept bees under lock-and-key, then issued further hives to other immigrants—franchises. But of course, if your company-bees are going to bring home decent honey, you *have* to let fly off loose, free all day. They'll soon branch out on you. They leave. You cannot hold them.

Angus had liked Maimie. He tried imagining how any employer might've treated her more justly. Accidents will happen, what the boys in insurance call 'acts of God'. Head lowered, he half-smiled: There'd been the first time Beech ever saw him come downstairs in full Scots regalia. She'd spied his kilt, she lost all usual dignified reserve. Beech clamped one hand over her mouth and giggled, pointing. Everybody laughed along with her. Angus—fists knuckled on his hips, feeling handsome and powerful and patient astride the third stairstep—grinned, "So, what *is* this I'm a-presently wearing, Maimie Beech?" (One reason you keep servants—getting their news of you, how they 'read' you.)

Beech answered, shy, pleased, "A diaper, a plaid diaper, and on a man!"

Suicide seemed so *unlike* her. 'Self warth,' he'd felt it—a solid floor-bid—living stubborn in and under his Miss Maimie. (Maybe she caught a disease from the aristocrats who'd hired her prior to Angus: they believed a person either had standing or had nothing-at-all.)

McCloud now asked hisself why he should always feel surprised when others disappointed him? He steadily searched the world for people with the kind of grit and springiness he'd had when young. He longed to find just one member of the deserving poor who was presently as poor and deserving as he'd been there on deck—skin and bones and rickets, but already planning, planning.

A first business-partner had told Angus he was a fine judge of others' characters—that he noticed everything but luck. Part of McCloud's own luck meant: barely admitting to luck's wild-child wild-card effect upon hisself, his fortunes. —That really *is* luck. Or is it?

But, the handsome fellow straightened now, no percentages in sulking, why dwell long on sadness? Just vanity, this hating to be wrong about your staff. Your sadness only burdened those around you. So Angus slid one arm along the pew-back, guarding the three homely gifted girls here on his right. Maybe they'd been unduly upset by the excess emotion pounding hereabouts: girls were crying as they'd never done (disappointing Angus) when their own little sister got so maimed.

Hedged by weeping and the handclaps here, McCloud determined to feel cheered. Yes, you made your own luck. He imagined that first hive set on open-deck, bound for the new land. Bugs had been silent during the six week crossing. Fed sugar-water from a pan, they seemed groggy from the rocking

and the salt-air. But, before even the keenest land-loving sailor
sensed a continent waiting forty miles ahead in fog, bees knew.
They smelled its fulness, the perfume. Nervous sailors gathered
—smiling—around a hive suddenly unsticking, groaning with
a churning life—wholly charming, totally menacing. Kidnapped
bugs sniffed it first: green profit dead-ahead.

Angus could so easily picture his Bianca alone at home now.
She'd be straight-backed before her new white Steinway. He had
never offered her anything but the earth's fullest and finest, its
choicest help.

And—for all the sadness of this Maimie-business—McCloud
supposed that, here too, if half-on-the-slant, he had somehow
managed. Again, he'd come out in the black. Maimie'd given
Angus what he *claimed* to want. Even from Beech, he'd got the
verra best.

So, sure: His youngest could be trusted alone at home for
the hour and a half one funeral'd take.

She was, after all, such a good little girl.

ALLAN GURGANUS was born in Rocky Mount, NC and — currently living in Manhattan — is glad of that. His short fiction has appeared in *The Atlantic, Harper's* and *The New Yorker.* He has won many fellowships and prizes including two grants from the National Endowment for the Arts. Gurganus' novel, titled *Oldest Living Confederate Widow Tells All,* will be published by Alfred A. Knopf. Chapters from the book have appeared in *The Paris Review, The Southwest Review* and *Antaeus.* He has just finished a collection of stories called *White People.* His paintings are represented in private and public collections including that of The North Carolina Museum of Art.

Gurganus has taught fiction writing at Stanford and Duke and is on the permanent staff at Sarah Lawrence College. This Fall he will teach at The Iowa Writers' Workshop. — 'Good Help' is a chapter from the forthcoming novel.

His teacher John Cheever wrote, "I consider Allan Gurganus the most morally responsive and technically brilliant writer of his generation."

Good Help was designed and composed by Bull City Studios, typeset by Azalea Typography, printed at Regulator Press, and bound and trimmed at Bull City Folder—all of Durham, North Carolina.

One thousand copies are signed, an additional twenty-six are lettered, signed and accompanied by an original drawing by the author.   **749**

Good Help

Patrons of the Edition